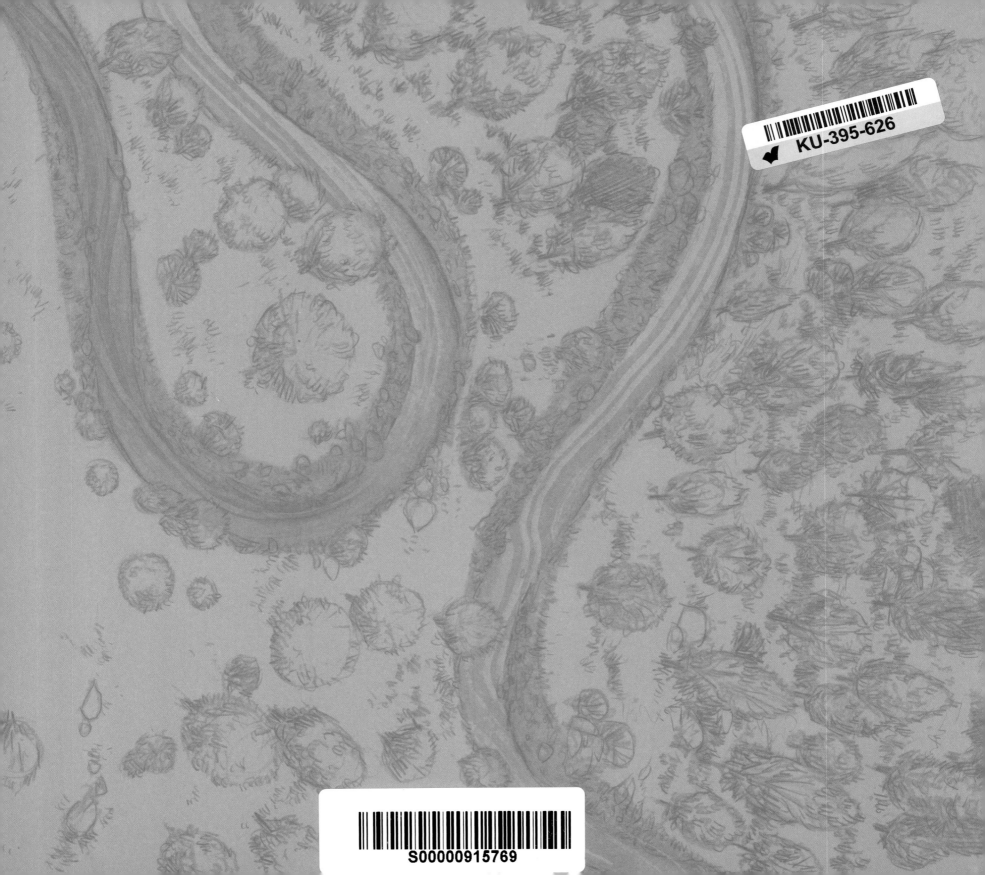

the Tree and the River

AARON BECKER

WALKER BOOKS

AND SUBSIDIARIES

LONDON • BOSTON • SYDNEY • AUCKLAND

*For Mary Lee, my trusted guide
through wordless worlds*

First published 2023 by Walker Books Ltd, 87 Vauxhall Walk, London SE11 5HJ
© 2023 Aaron Becker • The right of Aaron Becker to be identified as author of this work
has been asserted in accordance with the Copyright, Designs and Patents Act 1988
Printed in China • All rights reserved. No part of this book may be reproduced,
transmitted or stored in an information retrieval system in any form or by any means,
graphic, electronic or mechanical, including photocopying, taping and recording,
without prior written permission from the publisher. • British Library Cataloguing in
Publication Data: a catalogue record for this book is available from the British Library
ISBN 978-1-5295-1294-6 • www.walker.co.uk • 10 9 8 7 6 5 4 3 2 1

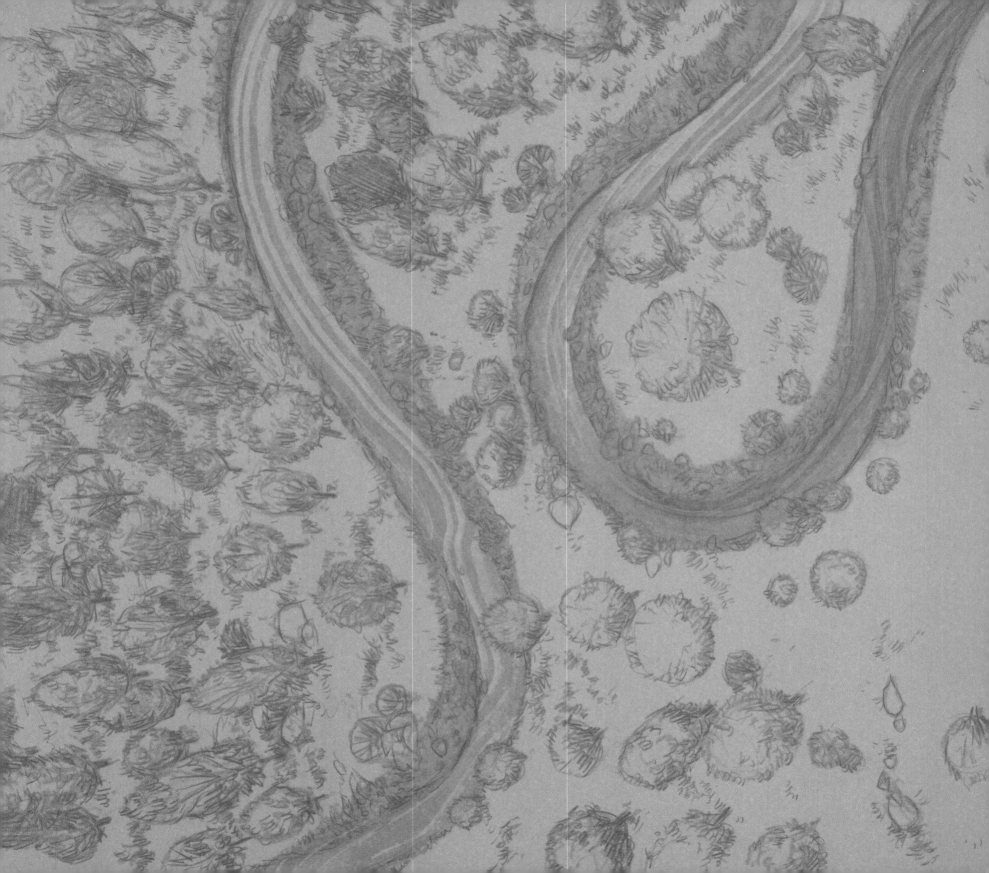